Selected Poems
of
Elliot M. Rubin

Vol. I

Preface

As a writer of thrilling five-star crime novels, I find poetry to be a reflective and rewarding enterprise.

Writing on a personal level in easy to understand the language, I want everyone to be able to enjoy my poems. I hope you experience the humanity I tried to express in many of these poems.

Although there are many styles and genres written here, some are humorous, and some serious, but all are from the heart.

Sometimes a creative person goes into their imagination and lives the thoughts in his mind as he puts them on paper. They are as real to me as if they occurred.

You do not need an advanced degree in literature to appreciate these poems.

I selected the poems in this collection to represent a varied spectrum of my writings.

Please enjoy them.

Table of Contents

Loss

Like spilled milk,

It's nutrients on the floor,

My mother's death

Leaves me malnourished

Red Ribbon

It is sitting on my bookshelf for decades,
  yet I never really noticed it until today.
The small, solitary red ribbon, innocently draped
  over the spine of a summer reading novel
I never finished

I bought it on the boardwalk in Asbury Park
 in the heat of a summer romance. I remember
as she untied her ponytail with this short ribbon,
  her hair cascaded down her back, and gently
brushed against my face

I placed the ribbon in the fold of my novel,
  innocently thinking it would be my summer
bookmark,
not knowing the single strand of red satin
  would hold numerous stories within its fibers,
to return forever in my memories

Sunset

The sunlight in my heart is dimming.
  I fight off despair with a two-edged sword,
Awaiting the outcome of my last big battle,
  Knowing for decades, this has been coming

The cutting edge of my defense,
  Is the love I have known for years,
It is my inspiration to fight on,
  For eternity is my enemy now

She is sitting beside my bed
  And holding my hand so gently,
I can feel her tears softly flowing
  And falling onto my arm

The midnight dark is fast approaching,
  My knowledge will be gone forever-
The years of toil and romance
  Are soon coming to an end

I am the sun, and my young planets are
  Floating around my bed, waiting
For the last flicker of light to expire;
  As with a supernova, I smile at them
one last time

You Left Me

You left me before I could say goodbye,
  I am lost without you at my side,
We knew someday this would be coming,
  You are the glue that bound us together

There are no words to express my love,
  It is unspoken, and runs deep in my soul,
My dreams were to have you here forever,
  To hold your hand as life goes on

All night I sat at your bedside,
  I closed my eyes for only a moment,
You slipped away without a sigh,
  I'll love you forever, and a day

A flower garden called Newtown

As the sun rose in the east,
The smallest buds perked up again,
Ready to start another day,
Of growing and absorbing

The warmth of the sun
Refreshed them, their
Hidden futures not ready to bloom.
The day had just begun

The earth awaited their blossoms,
The potential to grow assumed,
But a madman cut the buds off,
And the flower garden died

Janis

It was February nineteen sixty-nine.
  In the East Village, she was going to play,
I was walking along minding my business,
  When this crazy wild girl called out to me, *stop!*

She is standing still in a candy store door,
  When I turned and saw her smile out at me.
With stringy blond hair, and loose hippie clothes,
  Wearing cowboy boots and wooden love beads

I wore slacks, and a dark blue blazer,
  With curly hair and a boney frame,
She asked me if I wanted to party,
  Free love and booze, and Mary Jane

That afternoon I will never forget,
  No one believes me when I say,
I partied with her all night and day,
  Until she left to go rehearse

A National Disgrace

When he was eighteen, he joined the Marines
   To serve his country as best he could,
Through basic training and deployment overseas;
   He served in combat with pride and honor

Risking life and limb in a foreign land,
   Never doubting the orders, he is given,
He forged ahead in heart-throbbing battle,
   To return home, a shattered young man

There were no outward signs of harm.
   He had all his legs and use of arms,
The nighttime dreams caused a sweat
   When he awoke, his clothes were wet.

His mom brought him to the VA for help,
   They took his name and told him to wait.
Due to budget cuts, they could see him someday,
   Maybe six months, they told them to wait

That night at home, he walked outside,
   To the secluded part of his mom's backyard,
Then laid his pistol beside his leg,
   He took some pills to go to sleep

The officer folded the flag just right,
   Then handed it to his mom to keep.
A quick salute, and down he went,
   While politicians cut taxes for the very rich

Nothing left

The bleached desert floor is dry and cracked,
  Its lifeblood evaporated, and dead to all,
As far as the eye can see, there is empty,
  So similar to the love you had for me

The prickly thorns of the lonely cactus,
  Can't take any more from my empty veins,
My future is blank, and my past is shattered;
  You ripped the heart right out of me

I thought the heavens sent you down to earth.
  We smiled, and laughed, and danced together,
Every day was a blessing to be with you,
  Then out of nowhere, everything changed

The flames of hell swelled up so high,
  Satan's spawn seemed to reside with me,
Trapped with you my skin burnt up,
  I could not breathe, I had to leave

I loved you. I loved you, where did you go.
  I am lost and alone, and I miss you too much,
I don't know if I can go on in this life,
  I have nothing to live for,
    You put out my flame

Et Tu Brutus

Genuine trust is a scarce thing,
  It's extremely hard to find,
This is the bedrock, which binds a family.
  Value and hold it as you would a jewel

When a kin's trust betrays you,
  The cut goes deep in your heart.
There is no blood, and the wound does hurt,
  It never heals, and is there forever

Like the death of a loved one
  You feel depressed and abandoned.
The lifelong bond you felt is gone,
    Bitterness and grief are constant companions

After a Rain

Like a nervous person impatiently waiting,

  Tapping their fingers on a table or desk;

   The slow droplets of water ripple through my nerves,

    When hitting my window sill air conditioner,

     Irritating me to no end

Erev Hanukkah

Twas erve Hanukkah,
throughout the whole house,
Mom's brisket was cooking
permeating her blouse

the latkes were sizzling
our home smelled of oil,
we were shvitzing and tired
while the chickens did boil

there was no brick chimney
or old socks to fill,
the kinder sat motionless
by a cold windowsill

waiting for our Bubbe
to visit that night,
and Zayde to drive her
and then have a bite;
of Momma's home cooking,
egg noodles too,
with stuffed derma tummies
we were a full crew

then Uncle Moishe
parked his old battered van,
and out came our cousins
chalk-white with no tan

there is Yossie and Malka,
and Chaim with old Tante Fran,
then Channa, and Dovid,
with Schmuie and some unknown man

he was tall, and all wrinkled
with hair flaxen white,
his beard was so long
it seemed not to end

as he stepped out
he did need to bend,
then we saw fall
from his black woolen coat,
some letters and cards
we wrote and did send

to a Rebbe some questions,
just questions, to no end.
but he thought them good,
maybe, that will depend

so everyone did come
for dinner that night;
the Rebbe, the family,
the cousins, you see,
for on erev Hanukkah
there is no TV

the family came
not just for the food,
but to gather together
to joyously schmooze

A Shattered Life in Class

Sitting near us she started to speak
  About her life, and the sadness oozed
From her mouth with a tinge of bitterness;
  Impacting those of us who had no choice
But to sit and listen

I am reminded of an antique vase,
  With an aged patina from a life's experience,
As she told of her lost loves and tragedies;
  How well she thinks she is coping with them

There are micro cracks in the still beautiful vase-
  Glued back, piece by piece, till it somewhat
Resembles the original, seemingly unbroken.
  Yet as she spoke the damaged edges
Became apparent, to everyone except herself

In a Corner

At dusk one day as I walked home from work,
  I passed a side door in the dark, dank alley
Of a large, faded, old red-brick building
  Built-in the booming fifties after the war-
The cries of a young child caught my attention-
  Set back in the dark corner of a little-used entrance,
I saw curled up a seven-year-old sobbing,
  Into unwashed cupped hands held to its head,
And tears cascading down its arms-
  With delicate features, and a beautiful, gentle face,
  I could not tell if it was a boy or a girl.
  Close-cropped brown hair matted with dirt,
Unwashed clothes, stains, and soil easy to see-
  I hesitated to approach, afraid of being involved.
Yet the cries of a child echoed against the walls
  Crashing head-on into my heart; I asked
  why are you crying?
  I heard back *I am hungry, and only ate a piece of
bread since yesterday*
In a country of great wealth,
    I found a child living a third world existence,
bathed in poverty, a short bus ride away,
    From the wealth, and elegance, of snooty Park
Avenue-
I opened the takeout bag I bought for my dinner,
  Set it out with plastic knife, fork, and napkin,
Then sat on the concrete watching it be devoured,
  While I curled up and sobbed into my washed cupped
hands.

Unrequited Love

I am unsure of your reaction,
  If I told you that, I love you.
Will you return my genuine affection?
  Or break my heart into many small pieces?

I watched you from afar,
  We spoke a little once,
I don't think we'll ever join,
  I feel alone and insecure

We met in private places,
  A friend's home some weeks ago,
Our paths too often pass,
  It seems we always smile

At night I plan the future,
  A picket fence around our home,
But I am so much older,
  My heart is filled with doubt

You're alive and feeling vibrant,
  Jumping through life's events with youthful zest,
While I cherish a good night's sleep,
  And pray, I wake tomorrow

If I was a little bit younger,
  And you a bit more aged,
Our story would be written,
  They lived happily ever after

Belief

The wind can blow and fell a tree,
  It swoops down and removes my hat,
My face turns red from a gusty chill,
  I can't see it, but I know it's there

When I look into my grandchild's face,
  My heart beats a little faster,
Without touching it, my body feels
  Love exists, yet I cannot see it

There are some things we feel,
  There some things we do not see,
There are some things we do not understand,
  Yet we know they do exist

Recognition

My name has no meaning
  It does not stand for anything
Yet my soul cries out
  I am here; I am here

The Hunt

Buzz
I didn't get much sleep last night.

Buzz
All I heard was this sound in my ear.

Buzz
Turning on the lights, I hunted,

Buzz
My caveman within is rushing forth,

Buzz
To smite the beast seeking my blood,

Buzz
With curled up paper I look around,

Buzz
Until it lands on my lamp,

No more Buzz,
No more lamp,

Now more sleep?

The Decision

Being retired after fifty years of work,
and indecisive is not a fun place to be,
when considering if you should apply
for a new position at your age

Even if the money is right,
excellent really,
you must want to do it for sure,
or else forget it and move on

This is my decision;
to sit down,
and open
an ice-cold beer

Then to flip a coin
and heads, I apply

But then again,
sitting here with my beer,
maybe it's better
to let the world
float by.

If I work,
I would miss
the afternoon ballgame
on television

Ice Cream Cones

relationships are like ice cream cones,

a sweet taste when you begin,

and never enough to quite satisfy.

as you progress things get crunchy,

and then are left with nothing

but bittersweet memories

A Walk in Red Bank

today is a holiday and
the schools and banks are closed.
students are walking in packs
gliding down the sidewalk
as a mass of legs and heads,
talking in unfamiliar tongues,
although I know, it is English

as I turn the corner off Broad Street,
a young girl is walking by me,
tall and thin
wearing torn blue jeans at the knees,
and a loose tee shirt
on her slender body,
and smiles at me as we pass each other

I know the smile very well

it is the same smile
I gave my elderly aunt years ago,
as she sat on a chair amongst her friends
as I walked passed her sitting there

the girl's smile is a reminder
the circle of life goes on,
and someday a young person will see her,
and return the smile to her

Omissions can have Consequences

We have not spoken for almost one year

Last Valentine's Day
I gave her flowers and candy,
but did not tell her I love her

Now, I am alone

Nature

The locusts spring
onto the thorns
of the rose bush,
it's limbs shaking,
landing on its knees

Father, eating an apple,
sees sunlight on the
waters of a nearby pond,
with a field mouse
running on the green grass
of a manicured lawn

Mother is sitting under the trees,
notices the blades of grass move,
and throws a stone
at the bundle of leaves
piled in the distance

Who Likes Ballet?

They look like candlesticks standing straight,
rigid, no movement, boring to watch
until their arms float in the air,
gracefully, not showing
strain or effort. Muscular
legs lift up, and up, higher
yet, when they turn on point
with their arms over their
heads, hands touching,
twirling with grace, and
toes crunching. The
lead ballerina floats
across the stage
leaping into the
arms of a male
dancer who
catches her
mid-flight.
Holding the
prima ballerina
against his taut
body while he
glides across
the stage
the orchestra
plays, and
mirrors their
movements
in music on
point.
Wow
I love
it

Invisible

she is sitting
at the lunch table
by herself;
while cool kids
eat at the next one over,
ignoring her,
as if, she does not exist

lunch is peaceful
most of the time,
no one is making fun
of her today,
or saying cruel things
as kids, tend to do
occasionally

awkwardly tall
and thin,
not as socially developed
as her classmates,
although excelling
at her studies;
an honor student every year

at graduation
she is selected
valedictorian-
but turned it down;
didn't go to the ceremony

instead,
in her bedroom
she's staring up
at the ceiling;

blood slowly
dripping down
her wrist
onto the floor

going home

driving back
to my childhood home
for one last peek
at my long-past youth,
memories rush in,
bringing themselves
into my consciousness,
becoming aware
of their presence-
mentally seeing my friends
where we played
touch football
in front of our homes,
sewer cover to sewer cover
the line of scrimmage
is a glob of white spit
on black asphalt,
as we threw and ran the ball
all over the street;
never
stepping on streaks
of saliva
going from one goal
to the next,
making end run plays
or catches,
trying not to walk
on the starting line
as we counted
three Mississippi seconds
to start a play

standing
in front of my parents

former home,
i see the boys
of long ago
in my mind's eye;
sitting on the red brick stoop
talking
about subjects
of no importance today,
things I can't recall,
but were significant then

i vividly remember
teenage girls from school,
teenage girls, we played with,
teenage girls we dated,
all gone

dispersed into adulthood
like throwing seeds in the air,
carried away to mature elsewhere,
only to be imagined decades later
in my dreams and thoughts

bent twigs and wet feet

in the mountains of Vermont
high above a valley,
i walk along a path
with low undergrowth
as small twigs crack
under my feet,
inhaling
crisp, clean
unpolluted air-
far from the city;
letting my mind wander
aimlessly
with not a care in the world

a narrow creek ahead
is flowing fast, ponding in a crook

the sun is at its height
during summer,
heat melts my clothes
forcing me to visit
the cold freshwater,
getting my feet wet first-
sitting to cool off
as the icy current
splashes
on my back,
repeating and repeating
in a soothing pattern,
moving me
into a meditation
of mindlessness

still in my life

sometimes, they stay
talking and stirring
your mind,
forever in your life-
memories never leaving

some are youthful friends
or lusty past loves,
still tugging
at your emotions;
roiling your life

decades fly by so fast-
the future is finite,
the past is now the present-
ghosts can live with you forever

chocolate challah

the softness is sensual
  sweet to the taste,
    the braids are for gripping
    it's chocolate addictive
hand-rolled and baked
  waiting to be savored,
    the chocolate embedded
    then melted in the dough
one bite will tell you
  two will convince,
    the third is orgasmic
    you can't eat enough
they call it chocolate challah
  it's manna from heaven,
    this bet you will win
    it's better than cake!
no butter is needed
  or grape jelly too,
    everyone will love it
    and definitely you

miss you

when dark clouds
  in life
    bring me down

thinking of you
  makes the sun
    shine through

i can write
  a love poem,
    even with
      a broken heart

understanding

help me understand God;
things happen which
make no sense to me
nor to many others,
if you believe there is a God

help me understand God;
so many genocides took place
in the history books i don't
have enough fingers and toes
to count them all

help me understand God;
though terrible evil happens
people still believe there
is a merciful God,
who looks out for all

help me understand God;
all soldiers in war will tell you
God is in every foxhole,
yet is always on both sides-
with youth dying in combat

help me understand God;
why young children die,
innocents all, some stricken
with the worst diseases
or deformities possible?

help me understand God;
we attribute goods things
occurring to a heavenly
guide, but we don't know

why wickedness should exist
help me understand God;
we have free choice, yet
everything is preordained.
is the belief a comfort to our
mind when the end comes?

help me understand God!

a realization

standing on slimy
slippery moss
deep in the woods,
by the low bank
of a shallow
country creek,
crystal clear currents
gently collide
against a rock
jutting above the water,
stuck in the mud,
small air bubbles
permeating ripples
as small fish
flash by the stone

at the last second
they veer around
rocks and wood in their path,
avoiding a collision
by the smallest space
imaginable

caught in this cognitive moment,
i realize we are all like the fish

we go about our lives
as best we can,
trying to avoid disaster and harm
until we can't

trapped in the current of life

the bakery

the attractive display
in the window made me
stop, and look in the store
at the pastries under glass

the sugary swirls
on the sides of the cakes
brought my eyes up,
staring at the lone red cherry
with the long stem on top,
immersed in swirled whip cream
on a bed of chocolate waves

walking inside,
a pretty young woman
behind the counter
greets me
see anything you would like?

i liked her muffins,
but decided
i should not say
what i am thinking

i don't know her well enough yet
to ask for them in that manner;
but there is always the next tray
to bring out and see what's on it

after all, a bakery
is all about good taste

forgetting

i wanted to write

about forgetting,

but my thoughts

fled from my mind

broken glass

sitting on the edge
of the foyer table,
located between
candlesticks,
a framed picture of her,
the glass vase
seemed secure

until she threw a fit
slamming
the heavy door
on her way out

shaking the table
sending everything
crashing
to the floor

splintering glass
into a thousand
broken pieces,
like my heart

the moment

i am
the single red rose in a bushel of yellow,
the black dot on a white page,
a diamond surrounded by red rubies

i see
humor where others don't,
a story in an incident i witness,
creative fiction in reality

as a young boy
i daydreamed in elementary school,
i enjoyed listening to blues and jazz,
i purchased my first record -
Little Richard's Good Golly Miss Molly

looking back i am aware
of when the signs stood out,
but i did not understand them
at the time-

i was fourteen
growing up in a
stodgy,
conservative
middle-class area

walking past a shoe store
i spotted a pair of red,
patent-leather shoes
in the window,
and wanted them
against
my mother's protestations;

but they didn't have my size

that was the moment
i realized,
i was a unique individual-
the backward fork in the drawer,
about to march to the beat
of my own making
in life

urban princess

holding the hands of
two young children
while waiting in line,
the welfare office
is a jumble of bodies
wandering aimlessly
behind a screened counter,
looking busy,
yet the line
doesn't move

two visiting princes
promised her castles;
they are hit
and run royalty,
leaving
two new jewels
in their crown;
down for hours,
gone for years

the landlord wants her out,
section eight wants her in,
the twelve-month wait
places a princess on the street

her priests ban abortions,
her politicians banned them too,
her life is in ruins,
where are they now?

who's to help?

Spring flowers

i remember her
as a newlywed
leaving the house,
walking to the
farmers field
to pick wildflowers;
placing them
in a clear glass vase
filled with water
on the kitchen table
when she returned

the spring colors
of light blue with
pale yellow petals,
surrounded
by lavender florets
and green leaves
brightened the start
of every new day

the farm is gone,
overgrown
like weeds
with new homes
decades later,

she too has passed
into memory

leaving me with
an empty vase

like my life is now

the used book store

if you stand
in a tire store
the smell
of the rubber
permeates your brain,
giving you
a semi-high feeling
of euphoria

a used bookstore
sometimes
has a similar
smell,
one of knowledge
emanating from the
old tattered pages of
books stacked
on bending shelves,
under the weight
sitting on top

reaching for one
which caught my eye
i opened it.
it is a book
about a young family,
a sad book,
there are small
tear stains
on the margins
tugging
at my heart

on the inside

back cover
it seems like
a woman's handwriting,
she wrote a short note
saying the book is about
her parents;
please say a prayer
for them
when you finish
reading their story

closing the book
i purchased it

bringing it
to my apartment
to sit
on my bookshelf,
joining my family,
giving it a home again

discovery

in the car
before
kissing,
heavy breathing,
glazed eyes,
moonbeams
on naked skin,
love began;
then she knew-
no longer a virgin,
or heterosexual

truth

a writer
has to write the truth,
no matter how hard,
or if it hurts others
as well as themselves,
because truth matters

the Queen of England
goes through motions
to satisfy
politicians and public,
while she'd rather
ride in the fields
or cleaning her stables
with a shovel

the heroin addict
prostituting herself
at night to get a fix
regrets ever starting,
but has no way out
without help,
that is her truth

given facts,
real facts,
provable facts,
it is a writer's obligation
to let the sunshine
on the facts
come what may;
or truth
is not truth
anymore

elegy for my country

i mourn
the mighty imperial eagle
lying on the ground,
deadly talons
thrust in the air

once soaring high
amongst the clouds,
muscular wings
spread wide,
effortlessly
flying across miles
and miles

finally ending
as all empires do,
eaten by internal parasites
causing its demise

dead,
picked apart
by lowly animals
who once cowered
in fear

ghost wind

the barren
wheat field's
cut short,
harvested,
baled,
the combine
separates chaff
from seeds
spitting them out
onto a trailing truck

yet life continues
with the lone,
short daisy
standing tall;
its yellow petals
fluttering
in the ghost wind;
blowing invisible,
swaying the flower
back and forth
till planting
comes in Spring

when events
cut one down
and all is lost,
there is always
a ghost wind
to move you forward,
sometimes back,
but you are still there,
expecting tomorrow
to come again

glass

he walked out on her;
leaving a teenage marriage
of almost thirty years,
yet she was not upset

at work,
she smashed
glass ceilings,
working long hours,
playing hardball
with the boys upstairs

promotion after
promotion
till she reached
the top floor suite

the problem is
he loved her,
adored her;
yet could not
smash through the
glass wall she
placed between them

she outgrew him

mater lingua

i was born in this country-
English is my mother tongue,
Brooklynese is my
spoken language
of which I am quite fluent-
yet when talking, i do notice,
people crook their necks to listen;
cause i never diagram my sentences
mixing verbs, nouns, and subjects,
while ending with a proposition too-
grammar is not my strength,
or spelling for that matter, either.
i use woids not found too often,
with accents, not all comprehend.
so when you meet someone from
Brooklyn, listen, you'll understand,
even when we talk with our hands,
or sometimes our fingers!

1951

i was six, placed in the front seat
of my father's Hudson Hornet,
he drove the family to a working farm
for a summer away from the city;
with no air conditioning,
my stomach was turning,
i felt nauseated,
carsick, nothing to do but try
not to throw-up

my cousin and i played
in the fallow pastures,
inhaling the sweet aroma
of cut grass mixing in
with the piles of cow dung
scattered about

Schmidt's Farm in Middletown
was next to the race track.
on weekend nights we watched
mini Offenhauser race cars
scramble 'round the dirt-floored oval

next to the main field was a small
pasture, wedged between the track
and a forest; with a narrow path
leading to a freshwater creek
holding a pond in a crook of the flow

fish, frogs and small snakes swam
with us, and mother brought a
blanket for picnics under the trees,
away from the slimy green moss
where we would dry off and eat

one summer ending,
a small feline was brought
to guard the barn.
i played with it, a tiny, friendly
pussy cat; harmless and furry

next year it stood guard
by the barn door
when i came back;
the cat became a lion,
not approachable,
huge to my eyes, with
a stomach filled with rodents;
ending my last summer
on the farm.

New York Kismet

our eyes meet
for a breaths
duration

then you're gone

disappearing
walking up
the crowded
subway stairs

as my train
pulls out of
the station

nightlife

late at nightclubs,
booze flowing smooth,
girls at the bar,
pretty as a flower

bees buzzing 'round,
pants full of pollen,
looking for a petal
to pluck for the night

the choicest florets
always go first,
leaving the weeds
for the rest of the hive

the sad truth is
a pretty bright petal,
sometimes is bait
for a man-eating flower

floating 'round, the
butterflies swoop in,
sipping sweet nectar
bought by the bees

'til they get caught,
beautiful wings clipped,
innocence taken;
ending their night

a powerful storm

one day last year,
the weather channel
reported a massive storm
building over the ocean
and heading to shore

next evening
i walked to the boardwalk
and looked out to sea

in the distance,
i saw black and gray storm clouds
swirling on the horizon,
in a frantic dance over the ocean
while electric fingers stabbed down
igniting the sky at dusk

there are no ships to be seen
they are safe and secure in port
while the storm rages heading right at me

an hour later standing on the beach
the wind buffets my face

a drizzle is starting to fall,
water running down my neck,
soaking my shirt

high waves are racing to shore
raging with fury as they breach the beach
one after the other in a continuous assault

watching the surf crest and crash down on land
spattering onto the grains of sand

dissipating its strength,
reminds me of an elderly
prosperous and powerful person
who bulldozed their way through life
regardless of who was in the way;
and now is about to enter eternity,
equal to every other grain of sand

the next year on the very same day
i am sunning on the spot where i stood;
this time, it is sweat running down my neck, not rain;
and the storm, like the powerful, is forgotten

suicide relief

is suicide
a negative act?
ending the pain
is not a good thing?

your loss hurts those
who love you,
but does it bring
relief
from your demons
to others?

i don't know

writing

it is not easy to write
when autocorrect
corrects what it thinks
is correctable,
ignoring the intent
of a passage;
sending out incorrect
corrections
to make me seem
incoherent

this it does correctly!

clouds

i remember looking up
at the beautiful blue sky
while i held your hand,
and seeing white clouds waltz by
as they brought a peaceful smile
to your face

they seemed to hear a soft rhythm
as they casually passed overhead,
in contrast to the harsh grind of life
below, many of us must endure

yes, we had a good thing going

then the rain came
in a torrent,
sudden and severe
as we struggled to stay dry

you succumbed to the
dark gray storm clouds,
leaving me alone
and missing you

i can't look at the sky anymore
the clouds depress me,
and rampaging rivers now overflow
with the raindrops that fall from my eyes

parents

outside it is pouring rain and
lightning flashes blind me,
since your passing years ago
there are thunderstorms
in my heart

forever

since the beginning of time
it was grinding along
being crushed and shaped
below the earth's crust,
eventually, spat out and
exposed to the sun

it is now sitting
on the side of a country road,
a small elongated gray pebble
watching the world pass it by;
from its viewpoint
it seems very fast

yet its motion is none
until a young boy
walking by
picks it up,

skims it across a pond
watching it glide and hop along,
then sinking
among the fish and flora

its life in the sun has ended
never to be seen again

i remember her

we were only teenagers,
you were my sweetheart
to be mine forever and a day

with long brown hair
and a winning smile
how could I not love you?

i never could imagine not

you made the USA Teen finals,
a vibrant young girl
with star potential,
i was smitten,

but that was decades ago

i looked you up online one day
was disappointed in what i found.
you didn't mention children
or family, or friends
only an expensive luxury car

you showed no empathy
for people
or feelings of kindness to others,
only bragging

i am wiping my memory
clean of you,
clearly
i am disappointed

it is time for you to go

marriage

dating is similar to a rubber ball,
it can go fast,
sometimes   around-
            bouncing

it may take time
to slow down a bit;
until it finds
the perfect
resting
spot

    •

missed opportunity?

i did not like the way
she spoke to us

as a college student
i knew to keep quiet
and bite my tongue

i was there for an education

the next year she was fired
for sexual harassment
of her students

now I feel bad
i was not
attracted to her

moving on

it is hard
to forgive you
the hurt
runs deep

maybe in time
we can be together
again

but not now

i don't know why
you did it,
you know how much
i love you

what i need to do
is wipe clean
my feelings for you

i need an eraser

looking forward

i thought i would never say this

you have been with me
for so long
i can't remember
not having you always
at my side

yet nothing is forever

although i would like
to think otherwise
i need to deal
with reality

it is time for you to go

i loved my Brown Sugar,
for too many years
we were a couple

but my body
can't take you anymore,
at last, i am free
from your addiction

i threw away my needles

monster in the dark

late at night
i hear it roaming
around my ears
unseen in the darkness,
almost invisible
in the light

i know it is here

it's destiny in life
is to harass,
and tonight
it chose me

why?

what did i do
to this tiny monster
who wants my blood?

i gave at the Red Cross
support worthy charities
but no, it is not enough to warrant
a pass for a restful sleep

instead

i flip on the room lights
grab a rolled-up magazine
then start the hunt,
jumping on and off the bed
trying to clear the sleep from my eyes

it taunts me
flashing by my ears unobserved
then disappearing somewhere
in the room

waiting in ambush

the next morning i see it,
bloated
with my blood,
tired and resting
on the lip of the sink

awaiting its fate

summer romance

i've kissed you a hundred times
always with passion and love,
holding you gently in my arms
in an embrace which never ends

it was a summer romance
so many years ago,
teenagers with unchecked
emotions running wild

decades have passed,
i see you all the time;
then the morning arrives
and my dream always ends

with you
leaving me
once again

at a writers conference

i was mesmerized in class
while looking over her shoulder
from behind

at the notes, she is taking
while the lecturer speaks

in a small notebook
her words are hand-printed,
finely lined up and down the page,
perfectly level and evenly spaced

as if a mechanical printer did them

she is a faceless blond
in an aubergine blouse,
with her long hair twirling about
when she turns her head to lookup

how unique i find her writing

intimidated, i don't tell her
how much i am astounded
at what she is doing

there is no way in this life
i could ever do that

at best my printing
is similar to a kindergarten
child doing finger painting

i remain mesmerized

my problems are overbearing

the storm clouds
are coming at me
i can feel them in my bones

the darkness is pervasive
as i sink further
into myself.

in the last gasp effort
for help
i reached out to you

and you responded
with empathy
and love

thank you

i can feel
the sun
on my face
once again

witness

when i look at open fields
with overgrown green grass,
scattered about
are small
purple wildflowers
swaying with the wind;
i wonder why?

looking overhead there are
birds swooping down
effortlessly riding air currents
that i cannot see;
something is enabling them
i wonder what?

in a small bedroom
a mother cradles an infant,
the combined parts
of the baby is overwhelming
as they work together
to create a person,
i wonder how?

some people say it is nature,
some say it is the work of a god,
of which there are so many

i believe it is the work
of a source of power
we do not understand

to that source,
i am a witness

writing

unlike death

  writing never stops,

    until it is published

      …or re-edited

memories are hard to kill

they spring up when i
least expect them,
surprising me, and sometimes
they bring a smile to my face

it has been decades
since we were together;
kissing, holding tight,
and never thinking
of letting go

the other day i dreamt of you
as i was in a deep sleep

it was so real
i could feel
your breath
on my face

and i missed you
all over again

summer rain

massive storm clouds are rolling overhead

lightning and thunder shaking the house,

torrential rain is pounding the windows,

yet i feel safe and secure in your arms

the frost

summer is in the past,
with our running around
and playing together
in the water, memories
of time well spent

soon winter will be here
with the foraging critters
hibernating in the woods;
while we sit comfortably
in a heated home

as we look out at the
white crystals of ice
bending the green grass shafts
downward
with a gentle touch,
almost reaching the
cold frozen ground

the late fall frost
changed
the cheerful
summer colors
to brown,
awaiting a quilt
of white
yet to come

explaining

how do you explain
creativity to someone
with a plebian mind?

how do you explain
mental inspiration
to someone who
follows and
cannot inspire?

how do you explain
being different because
you have no choice?

how do you explain
there is no way to
explain these things?

enchantment at the bank

as i walked in the bank
this elderly white-haired lady
stood motionless
on the other side
of the glass door,
waiting

thin
blond
blue eyes
pink hair coiffed,
nice clothes
flirty eyes
flirty lips
flirty face

i open the door,
she smiles
at me asking
if i opened it
because of her
age or beauty?

i answer her,
both

it doesn't matter
if she is flirting
or not

it is years
too late
for me
to care

unrequited love

i'll be here to hold you up
if you ever crumble down

loving you from afar,
fearing rejection if i come too close,
exposing my heart to collapse
and my soul to humiliation,
leaves me on the sidelines
of love

in solitude

waiting for your call,

waiting forever,

waiting

for you to need me

squiggly lines

looking out the window after a rain
i see a small river of water
flowing fast,
just past my driveway,
pouring into the sewer drain
down the block

later the sun peeked out

i decided to go for a walk
when i noticed in front of
my door, under a portico,
a handful of squiggly lines
on the ice-cold grey concrete

not moving, still as death,
i looked at them

escaping from drenched
soil to high dry land,
the worms died trying to avoid death

not unlike
the women and children
coming here
to escape murderous
environments-
but killed or blocked
on their way to America
by untold dangers,
or by our border guards

when all they want
to do is live

her skin, her way, every way

the bright multi-colored floral tattoo
on her shoulder shouts out
to look at her,
not her body
in a skimpy two-piece swimsuit
running on the beach,
but at her shoulder,
the left one facing me
in the commercial, i am watching

years ago her body would be
the attraction for men,
but times have changed,
styles have changed,
attitudes have changed

today it is not the province
of only men to ink their bodies,
it is her skin, her way of expression,
her authority over her body
in more ways than one,
and nobody has the right
to tell her otherwise

especially
flaccid,
impotent,
older men;
whose virility
waned years ago,
still passing laws
about women's bodies

Saturday

what a miserable day it is,
high winds and whipping drizzle
blasting my face with torrential rain-
a typical fall weather day

gone are hot summer ones
with scantily clad girls
tanning on a beach towel-
with the sun smiling down

today i see them in warm coats
with a sweater underneath,
and a hat pulled down tight
against the driving wind

the best part of today
is when i woke up early,
flipped my eyes wide open
and had another day of life

a match made in Heaven

watching old black and white
Hollywood movies,
a glamorous platinum blond
is sitting on a plush velvet bench,
wearing an almost sheer negligée
taking out a fashionable cigarette case
and lighting one up,
inhaling a long,
drawn-out breath,
then exhaling gray smoke
for the camera to catch mid-air
as she turns her head,
smiling at the handsome leading man
standing in her bedroom
wearing a tuxedo

the reality both then and now
is not a fancy Beverly Hills mansion,
but a trailer home
somewhere in middle America
with a hungover brunette,
with tussled stringy hair
wearing an old,
stained
man's shirt
sitting in the middle
of a rumpled bed,
with a mangy looking dog
sleeping
on the linoleum floor
drooling

her guest for the night
is pulling on his pants

while looking for one shoe
while she asks
if you call me
we can go out again

they met last night at a bar,
danced, drank and shot pool together
till the wee hours of the morning

only to find himself
in her bed
when he awoke
as the sun shined in
through stained and torn
yellowed window shades

yes, of course, i'll call you;
what's your name again?

if Dr. Seuss wrote this poem

this poem is for the poet Bill,
i wrote it on a window sill

in the village of Poetsville
and counted every syllable

some write poems which rhyme,
some don't, not a crime

don't think i have the time,
think I'd rather mime!

early today

this morning
on my early walk
when the mist
gently kissed my face;
i decided to turn around
and go home, too wet outside

i couldn't see it
but felt the wetness

this made me uncomfortable;
not the morning chill
or the cloudy sky
but the minuscule beads
of moisture on my brow

in the warm comfort of home
i see on the news
thousands of mothers
marching slowly
hundreds of miles to America;
suckling their infants
in their arms
as they walk
in hope of a better life
for their children,
while carrying
all their possessions
on their back

i feel ashamed
to complain about
a light morning mist
on my face

funeral for Farley

the line of crows
are perched
on a tree limb-
high above the desolate
windblown cemetery
patiently waiting;
intently watching
two men below
digging deep
into the cold, hardened earth

the birds are hoping
for a frightened small mouse
to frantically dash out
of a safe earthen burrow
for their next meal

while i am tearfully holding a box of ashes
watching them
above and below
as I keep my long-time faithful companion
in my freezing hands
remembering his warmth

the only one in life
who gave me unconditional love
while i wait for the men to finish their work;
throwing shovel after shovel
over their broad shoulders
building a small mountain of fertile virgin soil

as the biting Autumn wind
pecked at my reddened cheeks;
i notice, nearby, red and gold leaves

clinging
as long as they can
to the tall
dappled
brown barked
denuded ornamental trees
as the short bushes above the graves
sway back and forth;
dancing on the rows of long-forgotten souls

finally letting go
of their tight grip under duress;
the lifeless leaves
float softly in the air
leaving their tree of life
as they are blown about
not in control of their destiny;
landing on the bottom
of the newly dug grave

making a colorful
thick
plush
bed of death
welcoming me in;
as i kneel
to place Farley's polished mahogany box
filled with his ashes
gently on them

sealing both their fates for eternity

one day's mail

quietly sitting on the grass
half asleep, he lifts his head
when the mail truck stutters
down the block;
stopping at every house

as the truck pulls up to his home
he stands, alert and watching,
as the uniformed postman
extends his hand out the window
to stuff letters in the mailbox

growling, exposing his teeth,
he lunges forward only to be stopped
by the grey chain link fence;
while the mail truck continues to lumber
to the next home a few feet away

satisfied he protected his turf
his muscles relax;
he sits on his favorite spot
below the tree,
then begins to lick himself;
and life goes on

absurdity

they go to church
praying to a god
who preaches
love,
charity,
and kindness to all

yet they want to
stop birth control
stop abortions
stop food stamps
stop welfare
stop free medical care

let them have their unwanted babies
let them worry about feeding them
let them watch kids get sick and die

because
they have a deficit to control
they have tax cuts to giveaway
they have to stop all "benefits."
they have a self-given righteousness

and on Sunday,
they have to go to church

the moth, the woman, and me

the bright flame of the candle
is intense and hot,
yet it draws the moth to it-
flying into the heat
not able to withdraw itself
from addiction like desire
to go into the light-
and prevent its demise

i notice a young woman
walk by me-
whose arms
are tattooed from wrists to shoulders
with multiple drawings in handcrafted colors;
a small silver ring pierced through her nose
and gold earrings outlining the ear-
with two
bright red,
thick,
pouty,
inviting lush lips
          beckoning me;
wearing tight
torn jeans
hugging her bee like curves,
accentuating
every movement with
every step she takes-
with tussled,
windblown,
long brown hair
flowing
down her back

i am drawn to her
wild girl image-
against all my intuition
and knowledge
gained from maturity
and marriage
not to approach her,
yet i do so willingly
not able to help myself;
i don't know why

a walk at night

'twas midnight black as pitch,
no one near muscles twitch,
clutching my phone ever so tight,
my nerves rattle from ghostly fright

i enter through a rust-covered gate,
creaking loud i decide to wait-
i look around at many small mounds
scattered all about on silent still grounds

the full moon tonight is at its height,
as church bells sound so out of breath
slowly once, twice, until all twelve tones
break the silence of eternal death

echoes of silence
  broken twelve times
    waking the dead
      from endless sleep

a dark shadow sits high,
watching the dead
then looks at me to turn its head,
giving me a black cat's sly eye

i see massive stones rigid as troops,
waiting for orders not moving at all-
i see in the distance, in the night,
a line of barren trees lonely and tall

they wait for a storm hard and severe,
for winds to uproot them, no one sheds a tear
when they fall to join the dead below;
another death, another life to flow-
their trunks are hollow, eaten by bugs
who travel up from the dead below

shadows drift up from a field not far,
gathering merrily as in a bar,
gliding in the air at a newly dug grave
where i stand; frozen in fear-
calling out, they disappear,
as if, never here

a short walk to where they prance
are shadows with eyes ever so bright,
filling my soul with deathly fright-
yet i stand in a cemetery at night,
where souls rise to dance merrily

i see a newly dug plot, not yet marked,
except for soldier's wreath laid on top-
dead and buried unknown to all,
except by those predeceased and on-call

they welcomed him home at midnight tonight,
lonely no more with old friends now found,
finally honored on hallowed ground,
remembered by all who fell before

senior Thursdays

she stops in the middle
of the aisle
blocking my path
   i notice her
   red, blue and pink
   floral dress,
   stylish thirty years ago

she looks at red apples
stacked one on top of the other
in a pyramid-
they are all the same color
with stems pointing up,
maybe a worm or two
drilling through a few,
when she turns
looking through the pile-
people are lined up
behind me
with empty carts
eager to be filled,
yet she is oblivious
to the world,
living in her reality-
someday that could be me,
with drool slowly
slithering down my chin
onto my shirt,
and a nurse
pushing me in a wheelchair
because it is Thursday,
trip day to the market

The Master at Dance

As I swept her off her feet
  With my smooth yet stylish moves,
The music continued to play,
  As we tangoed around the room

My arm gently encircled her waist,
  Our hands clasped and pointed east,
I led with my spirited charm and wit,
  As she dipped and held me close

A dance for lovers is what I told her.
  She smiled, and asked so softly,
Are you as experienced as the dance?
  So I held her ever closer

Others cleared the floor for us
  We twirled, spun, and circled 'round,
Lost in a moment of passion,
  We were in another world

The people on the edge are watching,
  Until our last spin and dip are done.
As I held her hand in mine, and
  Raised it to my mouth, she smiled,
And quietly asked my name

My legs felt weak and feeble,
  I could dance the night away,
But fumbled when I spoke to her,
  Now she is leading the dance of love

Other poetry books by Elliot M. Rubin

Scrambled Poems from my Heart
Aliyah, a poetic memoir
A Boutique Bouquet of Poems and Stories
bent twigs and wet feet
bits & pieces of free verse poetry
flash pan poetry
my life if I took another path
Rumblings of an Old Man
Stories of the South in prose poetry
Surf Avenue Girl
unrequited love

www.ingramcontent.com/pod-product-compliance
Lightning Source LLC
Chambersburg PA
CBHW060754180626
46818CB00002B/563